THE MESSY MONSTER BOOK

To Sabrina and Emil

Thanks to Emil Gordon Dauvois for the music

Thanks to Robert Paul and Sophie Dauvois

THE MESSY MONSTER BOOK

by Rachel Ortas

TATE PUBLISHING

Hello, I'm Messy Monster!

Jump into my book
and follow me.

Draw yourself here!

Meet my friends Zoe and Felix.

Get ready to use your imagination!

Hi, I'm Platoo. Together we are going
to think about things ... lots of things.

I am Doodle Cat. When you see me it's time to draw in the book!

I am Cutty Cat. We are going to make things together on a piece of paper outside of the book.

Messy Monster loves to play. He's great fun and loves to mess around.

Is your room in a jumble? Can't find your shoes? Are there holes in your socks? Maybe you have a Messy Monster in your bedroom!

'I love to keep things in my tummy. Eventually I give them back!'

'A really, really deep puddle!'

Help me draw an octopus.
Sometimes, what looks ugly to you will look beautiful to someone else. What do you think?
What a scary looking fish!
What a lovely looking fish!

Is it lying to tell imaginary stories?

'Almost there,' says Messy Monster.
'I can see it! Kiri Kiri Island!'

'Kirikiki kirikiki,' says Kiri.
'I have been waiting for you.'

'Kirikiki … We need your help …
Kirikiki … Terrible things are
happening on our island …
Kirikiki … We cannot dream
anymore, we only have
nightmares! We are afraid
to fall asleep … Kirikiki …
We are so tired!'

We are all scared of something.
Sometimes being scared is a good thing,
because it protects us from danger.

But sometimes we are scared of
things that can't even hurt us.
We are just scared of being scared!

'Kirikikikirikikikiki ...
 Will you help us, Messy Monster?'

'Of course!

It sounds like we need to visit the planet of the Dreaming Mountains.'

'Dandelions are fantastic
for flying into space!'

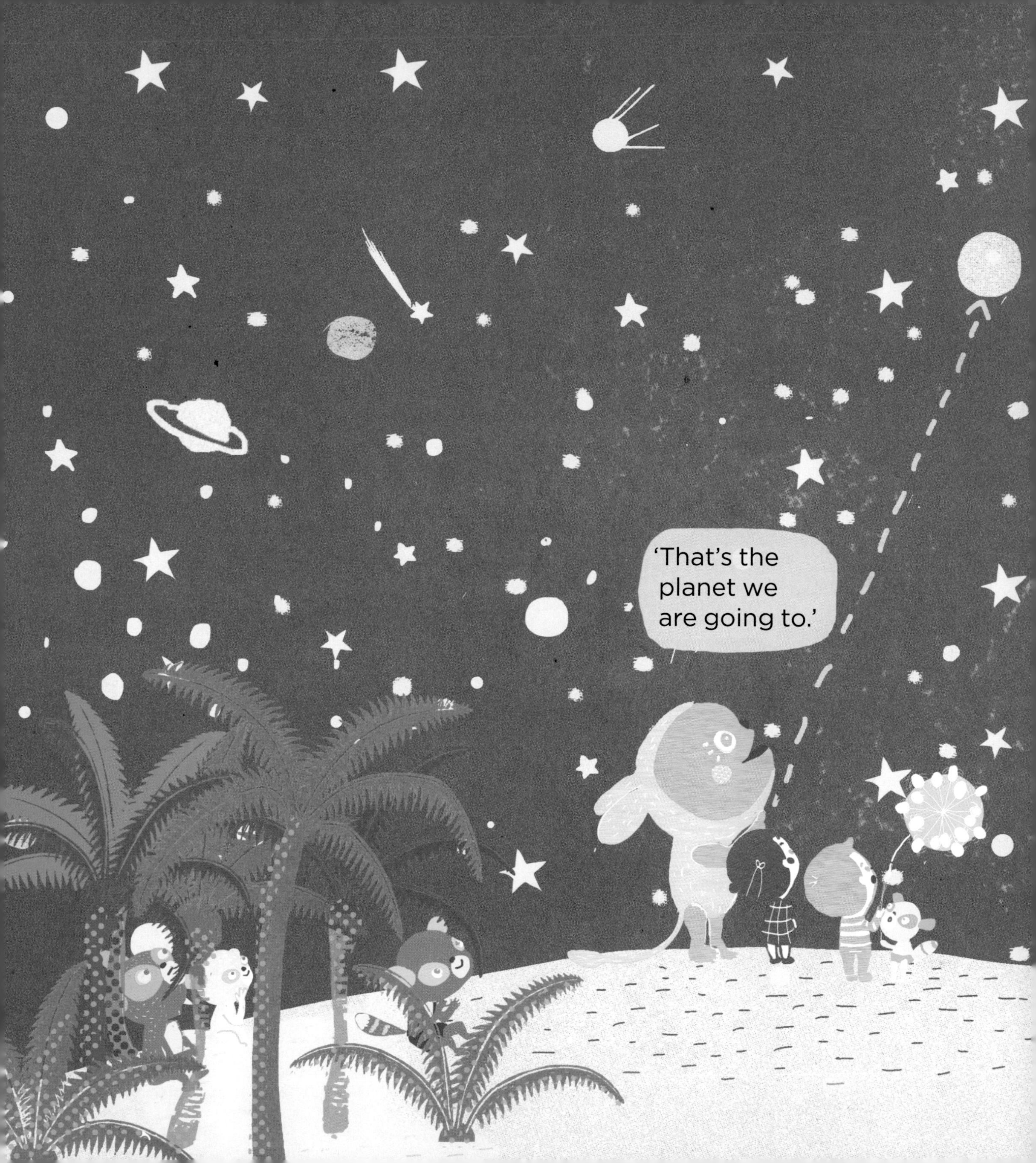
'That's the planet we are going to.'

'When I look at all the planets and stars in the sky I feel very small,' says Platoo. 'How about you?'

'Kirikiki ... Blow, wind, blow ...
all the way to the planet of
the Dreaming Mountains!'

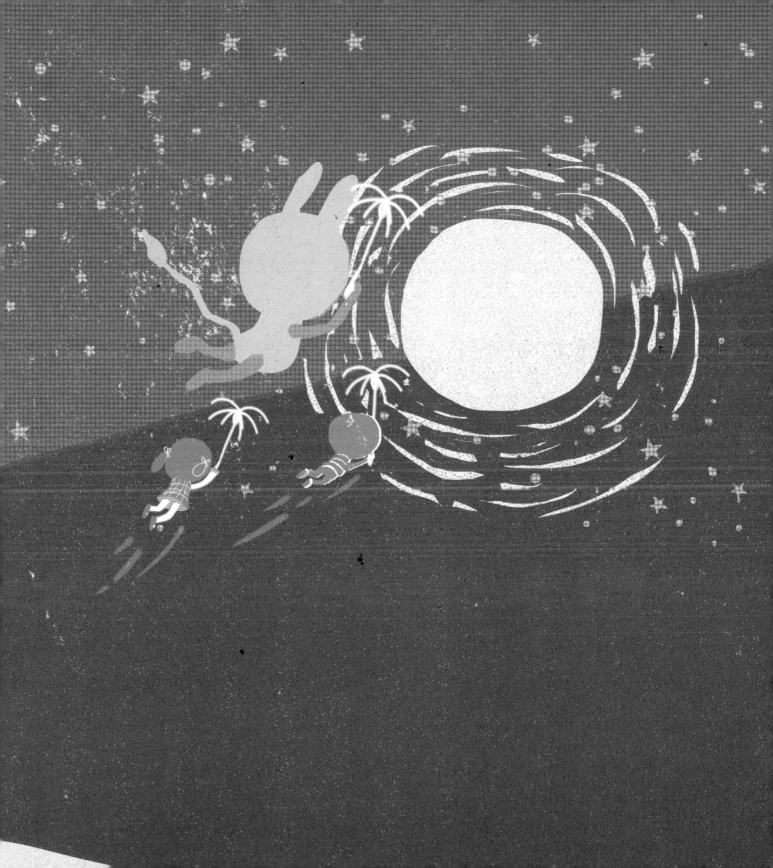

'Wind is very useful for travelling.'

'Get ready to land!'

'I'm scared,' says Felix.
'There are creepy things floating everywhere!'

'Don't be afraid,' says Messy Monster.
'They are only nightmares.'

'Look at the Dreaming Mountains,' says Messy Monster.

'Poor mountains!' says Zoe. 'They're having nightmares.'

Draw one of your nightmares here:

Draw one of your dreams here!

It's me, Cutty Cat. We are going to make a box to trap nightmares in.
Take a piece of paper and copy this design.

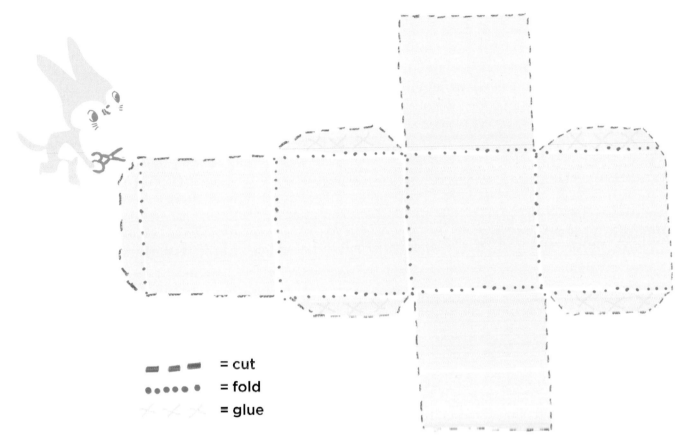

- - - = cut

•••••• = fold

✕ ✕ ✕ = glue

Whisper your nightmares into the box and close the lid. Once your nightmares are tucked away you will sleep peacefully all through the night.

'What can we do, Messy Monster?'

'We have to do something.
First we need to investigate,'
says Messy Monster.

'Ooh, it's a small fox. Hello Fox, can you help us?'

'No. Go away,' says the fox. 'I'm too sad. The music has gone and I miss it so much!'

'Oh look! This scrap of paper has musical notes on it! Let's sing Fox this song to see if we can cheer him up.'

'Little fox, little fox, little fox listen to our song,

Little fox, little fox, little fox, we are here as friends.'

What a lovely song!

There used to be music everywhere on this planet. Before the shadows came everything was beautiful, and only sweet dreams floated through the air.

But now there's no music and no musicians. The children in the orchestra ran away to the dark forest and became wild.

The dark forest is the only place the shadows cannot go.

'What terrifying shadows!'

Help Doodle Cat draw some nasty shadows!

'We will do our best to help you,' says Zoe.
'We are your friends!'

What is a friend?
Friends make us happy.

What do you think makes
a good friend?

On the Planet of the Dreaming Mountains

The mountains dream ...

... sweet dreams!

Nature feels the joy.

The muse dances.

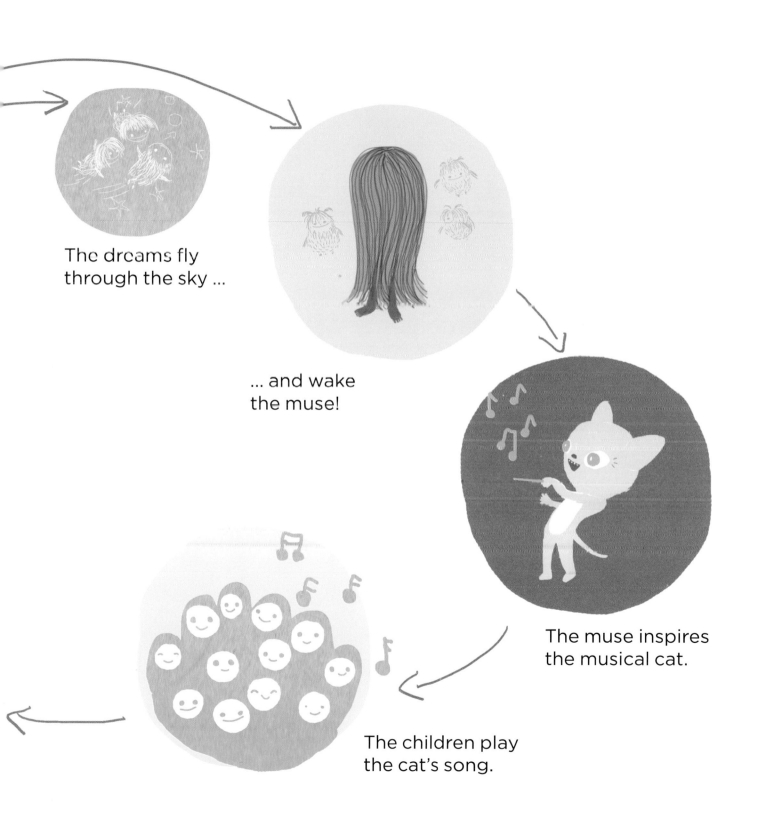

The dreams fly
through the sky ...

... and wake
the muse!

The muse inspires
the musical cat.

The children play
the cat's song.

What Happens When the Shadows Come!

The shadows appear.

They chase away the muse.

The nightmares spread throughout the galaxy.

The mountains have nightmares.

Nature wilts.

The muse disappears.

The musical cat
falls asleep.

The children run away ...

... and become wild.

'Bye
bye,
Fox.'

'Follow the tunnel and you
will find the dark forest,'
says the fox.

Can you see the wild children?

Luckily, Messy Monster has some stars in his tummy. Time to let them out!

'WOW!'

'We found the wild children!'

'Hey! It's Messy Monster,'
says a wild child.
'We thought you were just
in stories. Let's go wild!'

'It's fun to
go wild,'
says Zoe.

'This is fantastic,'
says Felix.

'How exciting to be wild!' says Felix.
'Do you have fun all day?'

'Not really,' answers the wild child.
'Sometimes all we do is argue.
 And we fight a lot.'

'We escaped the shadows in our baobab tree. It's our house and it looks after us too. It feeds us everyday and the fireflies give us light.'

'We found some musical notes.
They must belong to you.
Why don't you play some music?'

'No, no! We don't play music any more.
The musical cat has gone away.
Without him there is no orchestra.'

'I've got an idea for how we could bring the musical cat back. If we all play this tune on our Messy Monster Magic Whistles we might wake him up!'

Make a Messy Monster Magic Whistle with me!
All you need is paper and scissors.

'What a beautiful sound!
I remember now. I'm a
musical cat!'

'And I'm back!'

'Hello! Hello! It is so nice to see you all again,' says the musical cat.

'Thank you, Messy Monster. I'm so glad you came to wake me up!'

The musical cat tries to play ...
but something is missing.

'I've got an idea,' says Messy Monster.

Messy Monster starts to draw.

'A door!'

'Knock on the door and whatever you are missing will appear!'

Knock, knock!

Magic Dream Door

On a separate sheet of paper, draw a door. Cut along the
red dotted line. Stick the door on the wall next to your bed.
Knock on the door before you go to sleep and whoever
you miss will appear in your dreams!

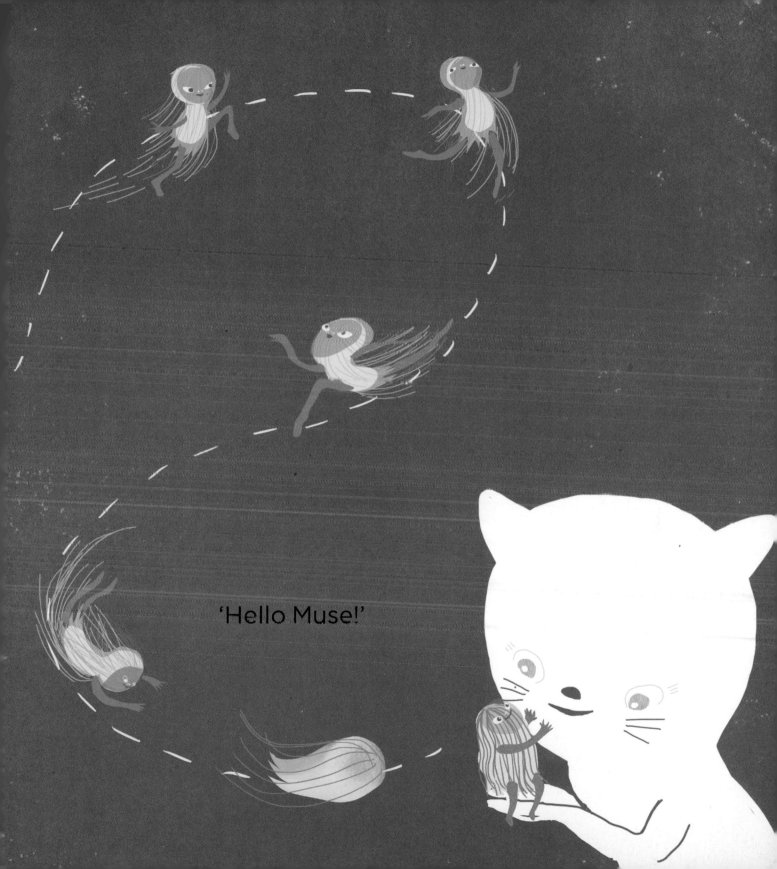

'Hello Muse!'

'It's time to get the orchestra back together,' says the musical cat.

'We like making music, but music practice is such hard work.'

'Once you get started it will
be so much fun,' says Zoe.

'You're right! We love
playing music together.'

'We kept your baton, Musical Cat.
Let's play!'

Sometimes it is worth
working hard to make
ourselves feel happy.
Do you agree?

Meanwhile ... Zoe, Felix and Messy Monster return to the Dreaming Mountains.

Messy Monster gulps
down all the shadows!

'Your tummy is
making strange
noises.'

RUMBLE!

Suddenly, Messy Monster starts to blow strange bubbles.
It's the shadows, but now they are all colourful and happy!

'Sorry, I've got to poo!'

'Oh! Flowers are growing from your poo, Messy Monster!'

Nothing really disappears. Everything changes into something new. Even beautiful things can grow from waste.

Written and illustrated by Rachel Ortas

First published 2014 by order of the Tate Trustees
by Tate Publishing, a division of Tate Enterprises Ltd,
Millbank, London SW1P 4RG
www.tate.org.uk/publishing

A catalogue record for this book is available
from the British Library
ISBN 978-1-84976-105-5
Distributed in the United States and Canada
by ABRAMS, New York
Library of Congress Control Number: 2013949979

Designed by Maria Spann
Colour reproduction by Grafos S.A.
Printed in Spain by Grafos S.A.

MIX
Paper from
responsible sources
FSC® C118858

Printed on sustainably sourced, certified paper